FOR AVERY, WITH LOVE —K.D.

FOR MY CHOSEN FAMILY AND BIPOC
QUEER-TRANS COMMUNITY. THANK YOU FOR
TRULY MODELING WHAT IT MEANS TO EVOLVE,
BE OUR AUTHENTIC SELVES IN MULTITUDES,
AND LOVE DEEPLY WITHOUT FEAR. —L.W.

THIS IS A BORZOI BOOK PUBLISHED BY ALFRED A. KNOPF

Text copyright © 2023 by Kelly DiPucchio
Illustrations copyright © 2023 by Loveis Wise

All rights reserved. Published in the United States by Alfred A. Knopf,
an imprint of Random House Children's Books,
a division of Penguin Random House LLC, New York.

Knopf, Borzoi Books, and the colophon are registered trademarks
of Penguin Random House LLC.

Visit us on the Web! rhcbooks.com

Educators and librarians, for a variety of teaching tools,
visit us at RHTeachersLibrarians.com

Library of Congress Cataloging-in-Publication Data is available upon request.
ISBN 978-0-593-42904-4 (trade) — ISBN 978-0-593-42905-1 (lib. bdg.) —
ISBN 978-0-593-42906-8 (ebook)

The text of this book is set in 16-point Ionic No 5 Medium.
The illustrations were created using Photoshop & Procreate.
Book design by Rachael Cole

MANUFACTURED IN CHINA
10 9 8 7 6 5 4 3 2 1
First Edition

BECOMING CHARLEY

WRITTEN BY **KELLY DiPUCCHIO**

ILLUSTRATED BY **LOVEIS WISE**

ALFRED A. KNOPF  NEW YORK

The forest was alive with young caterpillars who kept their heads down, eating, just as they'd been taught to do.

But not Charley.

Charley

looked

up.

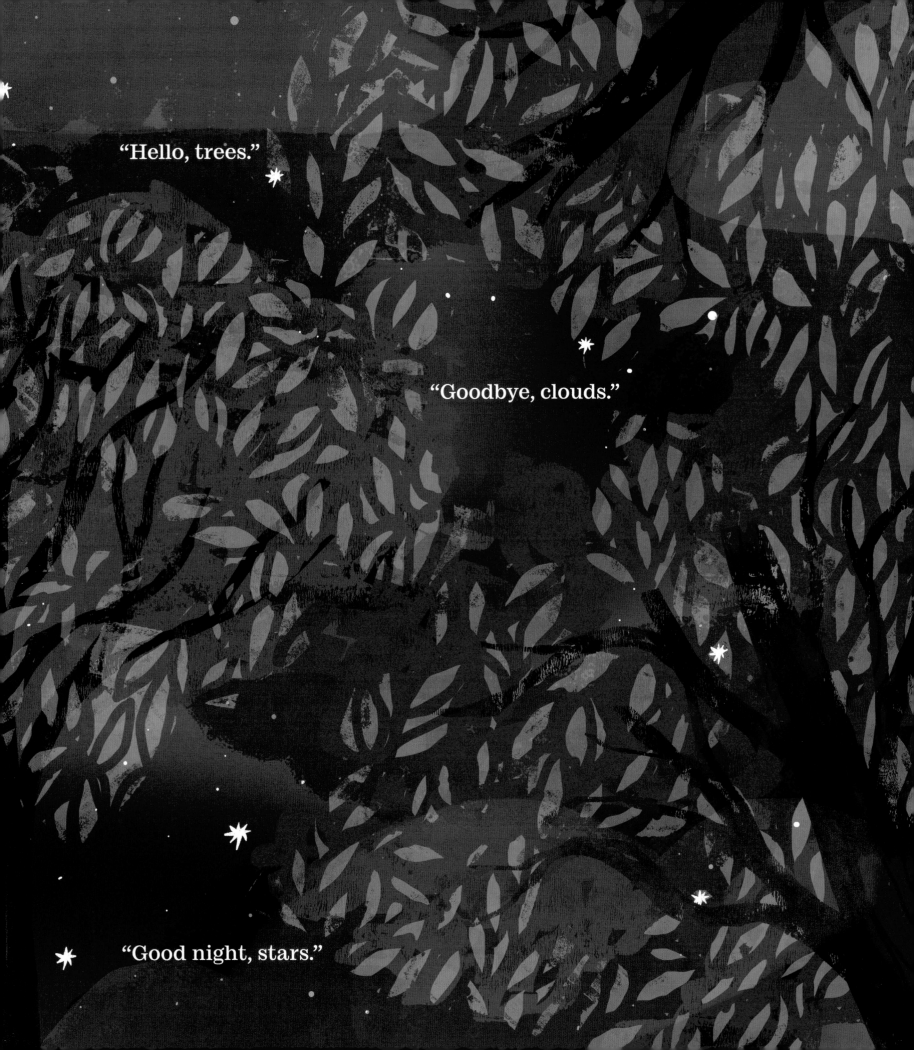

"*Charley!*" an elder scolded.

"Eat your milkweed!"

"You want to grow up to be a big, strong
butterfly, don't you?" said another.

Charley hadn't decided.

It might be nice to be a spotted fawn.

Or a waterfall.

Wouldn't that be fun?

During morning lessons, the young caterpillars were taught everything they needed to know about becoming a butterfly.

THINK BLACK.
THINK ORANGE.
THINK BLACK.
THINK ORANGE.

During afternoon lessons, they studied patterns and shapes.

THIS

NO

YES

UHN~ UHN

This.

Not that!

OKAY

NOPE

VERY
GOOD

NOT
THIS

This.

Not that!

Charley tried to concentrate on the
colors and shapes, but the sun beckoned.
"Over here!" she beamed, pointing out
new things to discover.

Wildflowers.

Mountains.

The turquoise sea.

"*CHARLEY!* Pay attention!"

BLACK. ORANGE.
THIS.
NOT THAT.

Charley listened until a leaf curled into a smile, inviting the young caterpillar to play.

Soon it was time for the caterpillars to form their chrysalis. Everyone was excited!

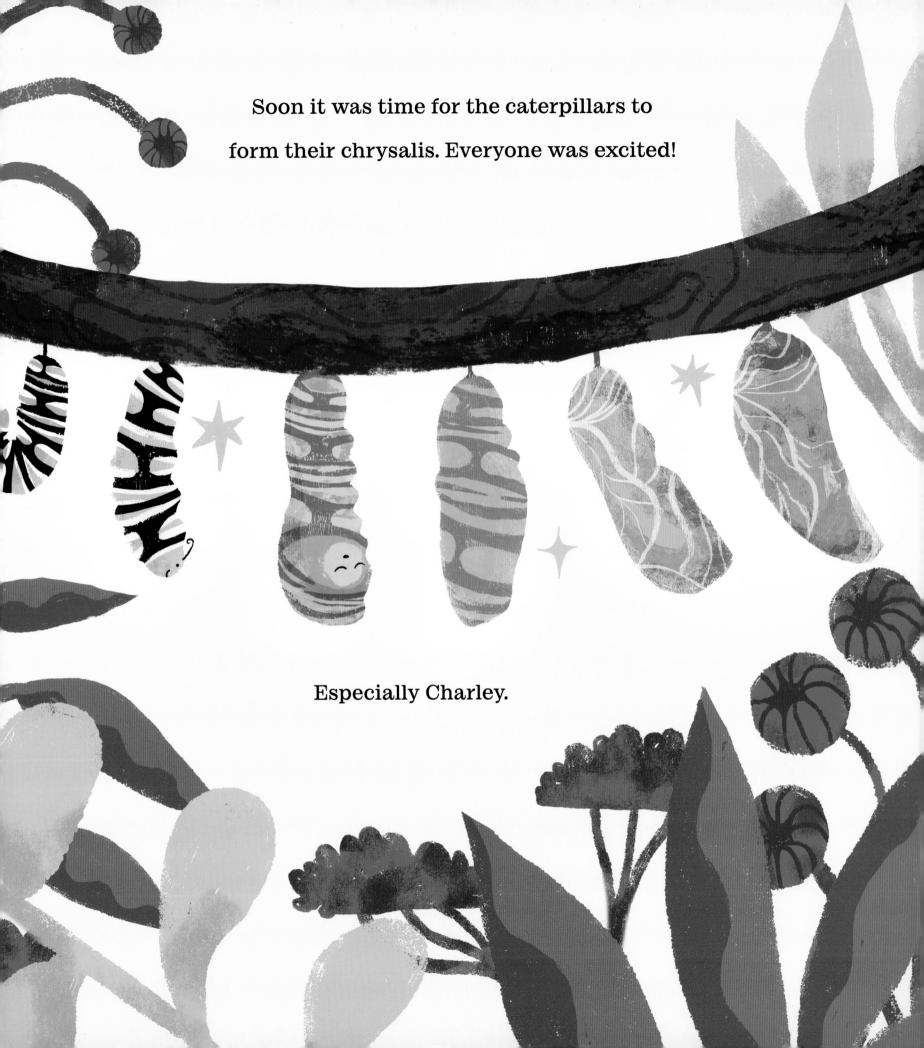

Especially Charley.

But once tucked inside the darkness, Charley felt unsure.

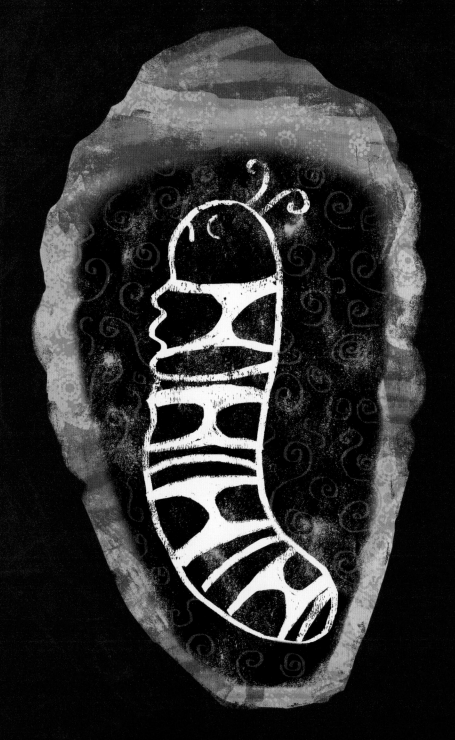

What came next?

Charley couldn't remember.

"THINK, CHARLEY, THINK!"

the caterpillar urged.

THINK BLACK.
THINK ORANGE.

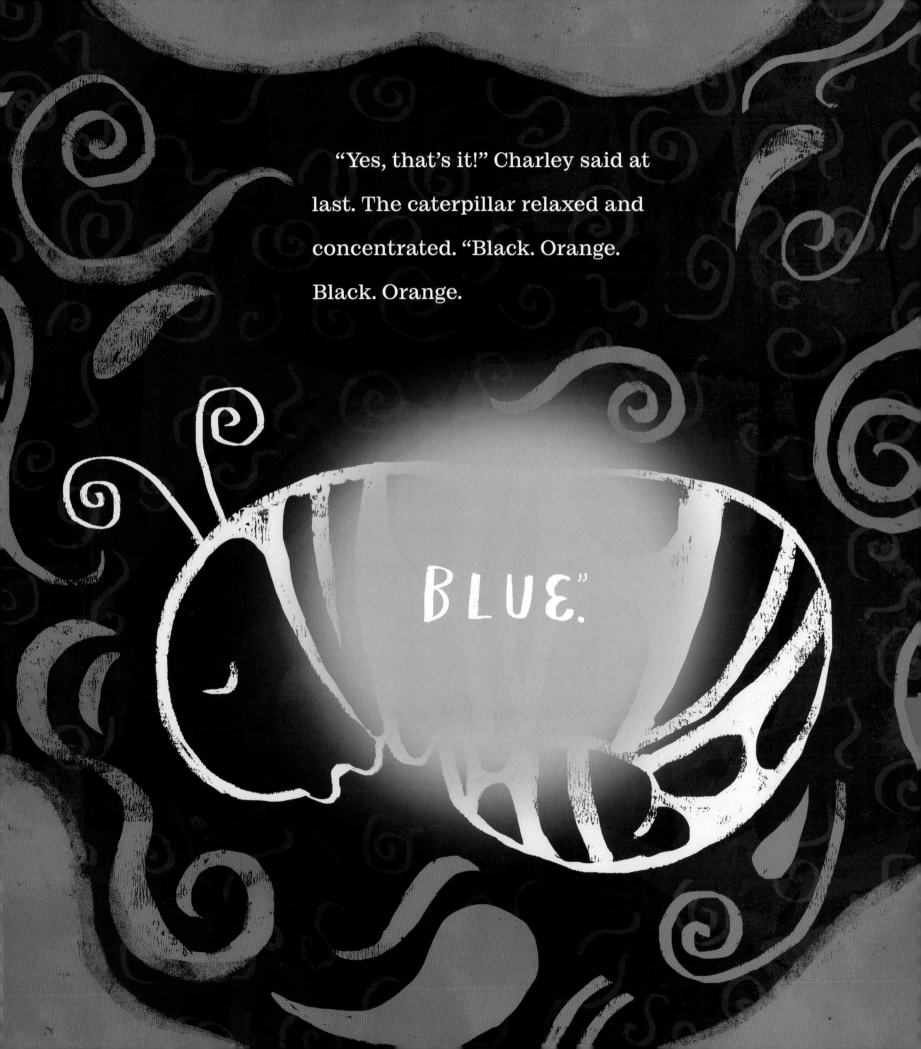

"Yes, that's it!" Charley said at last. The caterpillar relaxed and concentrated. "Black. Orange. Black. Orange.

BLUE."

BLUE?

Charley heard a bluebird singing in the distance.

The birdsong reminded the caterpillar of the trees

and the wildflowers and the turquoise sea.

Charley smiled and felt the peaceful
warmth of the sun. Now the caterpillar's
sleepy thoughts drifted back to the stars
and the clouds and the mountains. . . .

The summer fruits began to ripen, and the young butterflies woke from their slumber. Millions of butterflies dotted the sky like orange and black kites!

But which one was Charley?

Where was Charley?

Charley's tiny home remained still as a stone.

"I'm not surprised," said an elder with a frown.

"What a shame," said another.

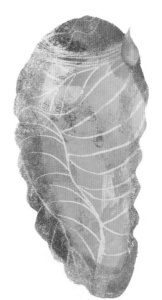

Just then, a single sip of dew landed on Charley's shell.

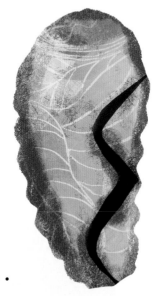

It stirred and shifted . . .

and cracked open.

Another butterfly emerged and took flight!

Only, this one was a little different from the rest.

Unlike the other young butterflies . . .

THIS
ONE
HAD
BECOME

EVERYTHING CHARLEY HAD EVER LOVED.